the twin
PRINCES

Tedd Arnold

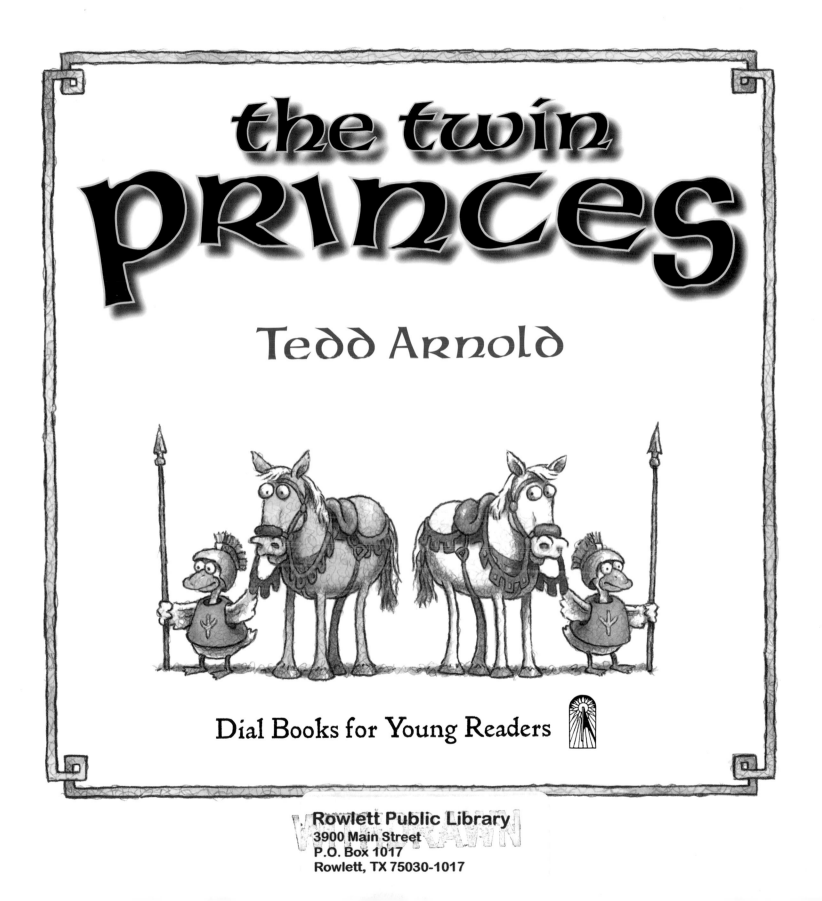

Dial Books for Young Readers

To my brothers, Bill, Chuck, and Dan, no twins among us,
in memory of our father, who told us this riddle-story

There's a riddle
in this story.
Can you solve it
before the end?

DIAL BOOKS FOR YOUNG READERS, A division of Penguin Young Readers Group, Published by The Penguin Group, Penguin Group (USA) Inc., 375 Hudson Street, New York, NY 10014, U.S.A., Penguin Group (Canada), 90 Eglinton Avenue East, Suite 700, Toronto, Ontario, Canada M4P 2Y3 (a division of Pearson Penguin Canada Inc.), Penguin Books Ltd, 80 Strand, London WC2R 0RL, England, Penguin Ireland, 25 St. Stephen's Green, Dublin 2, Ireland (a division of Penguin Books Ltd), Penguin Group (Australia), 250 Camberwell Road, Camberwell, Victoria 3124, Australia (a division of Pearson Australia Group Pty Ltd), Penguin Books India Pvt Ltd, 11 Community Centre, Panchsheel Park, New Delhi - 110 017, India, Penguin Group (NZ), Cnr Airborne and Rosedale Roads, Albany, Auckland 1310, New Zealand (a division of Pearson New Zealand Ltd), Penguin Books (South Africa) (Pty) Ltd, 24 Sturdee Avenue, Rosebank, Johannesburg 2196, South Africa, Penguin Books Ltd, Registered Offices: 80 Strand, London WC2R 0RL, England.

Typography by Nancy R. Leo-Kelly • Text set in Morris Golden • Manufactured in China on acid-free paper
1 3 5 7 9 10 8 6 4 2

Library of Congress Cataloging-in-Publication Data
Arnold, Tedd. The twin princes / Tedd Arnold. p.   cm.
Summary: Two chicken princes who are twins take part in a contest to determine which one will inherit the throne.
ISBN 978-0-8037-2696-3 [1. Chickens–Fiction. 2. Twins–Fiction. 3. Princes–Fiction.] I. Title. PZ7.A7379 Twi 2007   [E]–dc22   2005013300

The artwork was prepared with watercolor washes and colored pencils.

"Riddle me this . . ." the old nursemaid said.

"A story!" cried Henny.

Penny came running. "Yes! Tell us!"

The nursemaid chuckled. "Settle your feather dusters, and not another peep." Then she began again, "Riddle me this . . ."

Why did Old King Chanticleer worry about his two sons? They were both, as far as he could tell, perfect princes. Each was handsome, strong, and skilled in princely ways. Yet Chanticleer brooded over them more each day. Why? Because they were twins, and he could not decide which prince should inherit his throne.

Their mother, the queen, had died while birthing Henry and Fowler. In the confusion and grief after her death, the poor midwife lost track of which prince was born first. She was banished from the court.

Chanticleer loved his sons, but he was forever busy ruling the kingdom. While Henry and Fowler grew, he never had time for them. Indeed, he barely knew them.

How could he now choose between them? Finally, late one night, a new thought gave the old king hope. His yearly hunting expedition was set to begin the next day. For the first time, he would take his twin sons. Perhaps, during the hunt, one prince might prove himself more worthy to one day wear the crown.

In the morning, before the hunt, Henry and Fowler saddled their steeds, as they often did, for a race around the city.

"Last one back is a rotten egg," said Henry.

Fowler screeched, "Go!"

They charged from the gate, hooves and feathers flying. At a turn in the road, Henry began to take the lead. But Fowler cackled, "Cock-a-toodle-oo, dear brother," and he took a shortcut through the market, despite the peddlers in his way.

Henry saw what Fowler had done. He stopped to help an old woman who had nearly been trampled. Gathering her trinkets, he said, "I am sorry about my brother."

The old woman eyed him, then answered, "You crossed the road to help me. Please take this in return." She gave him a tiny carved horse and rider painted in Henry's royal purple.

Henry rode on alone. His brother's foul play was nothing new. Today a shortcut. Yesterday ants in his saddle. Each time they raced, Fowler hatched some scheme to beat him. But Henry kept racing because he simply loved to ride.

Back at the gates, Fowler waited. "Poor dear brother," he twittered. "You're not the early bird today."

Unruffled, Henry said, "We'll soon see who catches the worm."

The time arrived for the hunt. The entire city turned out to watch King Chanticleer lead the royal procession through the city gates.

The hunting party was deep within the forest when King Chanticleer spied a worthy prey. He sounded the hunting horn and charged.

The princes joined the chase. Fowler saw Henry taking the lead. "Have you forgotten your place in the pecking order?" he clucked, and yanked on Henry's cloak. Henry clutched the reins to keep from falling. His horse whinnied and stopped. "Cock-a-toodle-oo, dear brother," said Fowler.

Fowler's words caused his father to glance back. Chanticleer never saw the low-hanging branch that plucked him from his saddle.

Henry and Fowler watched helplessly as their father toppled to the ground. They flew to his side.

The king croaked in pain. "I fear for my life," he told his sons. "The next king must be chosen quickly. Tomorrow morning a horse race will decide which of you will inherit the throne."

Tents were pitched, nests were feathered, and Chanticleer was made comfortable. Henry stayed with his father all night.

Fowler paced outside. His only concern was how to win the upcoming race. At last, he had an idea. By the light of the moon, Fowler gathered poisonous henbane. He fed it to Henry's horse and chuckled to himself. "It is I who will one day rule the roost!"

In the morning, Fowler joined Henry at their father's side. The king looked at each of his sons, then spoke. "Our kingdom's future depends on this horse race. So let it be no ordinary race. Mark well my words. The brother whose horse is *last* to enter the city gates shall be the next king."

Fowler was furious. "The *last* horse wins?" he squawked. "Surely, Father, your wits have been scrambled by your fall!" Feathers flew when he stormed out of the tent and spurred his horse away.

Henry wanted only to stay with his injured father. But dutifully, he climbed into the saddle. When he realized his horse was sick, he dismounted. "This must be Fowler's doing," he muttered as they began a slow walk back to the city.

Hours passed before Henry emerged from the forest. Beside the road his brother was perched on a rock overlooking the city gates. "For once, dear brother, you may go first," Fowler said.

"Oh, no," replied Henry. "You go ahead, as always."

"I knew it!" Fowler groused. "There's no way to finish this featherbrained race. If I ride through the gates first, your horse will be last and you will become the next king. And even *you* aren't foolish enough to go first and make *me* king!"

Before you turn this page and find a clue, can you solve the riddle of the race?

"It is certainly a riddle," Henry agreed.

They were so perplexed that neither prince saw the old peddler woman until she stood beside them and spoke. "Messengers came to the city with news of your curious race."

"Who cares?" Fowler shouted. "Begone, old biddy!"

Instead of leaving, she examined Henry's horse and eyed Fowler suspiciously. Then from her tray she gave each prince a trinket. Fowler tossed his away without a glance.

Henry looked at what the woman had handed him—another carved horse and rider. He pulled the first one from his pocket. The new carving wasn't quite the same. The rider was again purple, but this horse was orange.

"I know how to finish the race," Henry announced.

Last chance to solve the riddle on your own before turning the page!

"Then share your wisdom," Fowler demanded.

"It's simple, really," said Henry. "We switch horses. If I ride your horse in first, my horse will be last. I will become the next king. And the same for you if you ride my horse in first."

"Well done!" said Fowler. He leaped onto Henry's horse. Too late, he remembered the poisonous henbane. "But your horse is sick!"

"Whose fault is that?" Henry answered as he hopped onto Fowler's horse. "Cock-a-toodle-oo, dear brother!"

Henry rode Fowler's horse through the city gates first, causing his own horse to enter last. Henry was declared the future king.

Old King Chanticleer did not die from his accident, but reigned happily for many more years. When at last Henry was crowned, Fowler flew the coop. King Henry's first decree was to restore the old midwife to her proper place in the court . . .

"That's you!" Henny and Penny interrupted, hugging their nursemaid.

The old midwife smiled. "So it is! Now, let me finish. Henry ruled his kingdom with fairness and wisdom. He married a beautiful princess and together they raised two lovely children."

"That's us!" Prince Henry and Princess Penelope chirped.

"Yes, and with you two," the nursemaid added, "King Henry and your mother will live happily ever after."